P9-DWI-085

THE CLUE IN THE
RECYCLING BIN

created by

GERTRUDE CHANDLER WARNER

Illustrated by Robert Papp

ALBERT WHITMAN & Company
Chicago, Illinois

Printed in the United States of America
10 9 8 7 6 5 4 3 2 LB 22 21 20 19 18 17

Illustrated by Robert Papp

Visit the Boxcar Children online at www.boxcarchildren.com.
For more information about Albert Whitman & Company,
visit our website at www.albertwhitman.com.

Contents

THE CLUE IN THE
RECYCLING BIN

CHAPTER 1

Treasures Everywhere

"Oh," said Violet. "Mrs. McGregor needs help." Violet, who was ten years old and a bit shy, opened the screen door to let Mrs. Mc-Gregor into the sunporch.

"Thank you, Violet," said Mrs. McGregor as she squeezed through the opening, cradling a big green object in her arms.

At closer look, Henry saw that the big green thing was a metal frog. He guessed that the frog was heavy, so he took it from Mrs. McGregor. At fourteen, Henry was the oldest of the four Alden children. "What would you like me to do with this?" he asked.

"Oh, thank you, Henry," said Mrs. McGregor, the cook and housekeeper. She worked for James Alden, the children's grandfather and guardian. "How do you think it would look if we put it here, on the floor of the sunporch?"

Henry put the frog down and stepped back to look at it.

"It looks very good," said twelve-year-old Jessie. "Where did you get it?"

Mrs. McGregor smiled. "I rescued it from the new recycling center that opened last week."

"Rescued?" asked Benny, who was six years old. "Was the frog in trouble?"

"No," laughed Mrs. McGregor. "The manager of the new recycling center puts a few things alongside her shed each morning— things she thinks can be reused. When I took my recycling in this morning, I saw this frog alongside the shed. Kayla, the manager, told me I should feel free to take it and reuse it."

Mrs. McGregor stepped back to look at the big metal animal. "Hmmm," she said. "I really liked the color of this frog when I saw it. But now I'm not exactly sure how we can reuse this frog."

"I know!" said Benny. "It's so big, it can guard our sunporch!"

Henry, Jessie, and Violet laughed.

"We already have Watch," said Jessie. Watch was the dog the Aldens had found and taken in. After their parents had died, the four children ran away and lived in an old boxcar in the woods. They ran away because their grandfather, whom they had never met, was going to be their guardian. They thought he would be a mean person. They turned out to be wrong: Their grandfather was a good person. He found them and brought them to live with him.

"Well," said Mrs. McGregor as she patted the large metal frog, "the frog can help Watch watch. And now it's time for me to make breakfast."

As the children helped Mrs. McGregor by

setting the table, they talked about the new recycling center.

"Does it take newspapers and cans and plastic?" asked Jessie.

"Yes, it does," said Mrs. McGregor.

"What's this I hear?" asked Grandfather as he walked into the kitchen.

"There's a new recycling center right here in Greenfield," answered Henry. "And it takes newspapers and cans and plastic bottles."

"That's wonderful," said Grandfather. "That means I don't have to drive the newspapers to Silver City and the cans and plastics to Elmford. That will mean less use of gasoline."

Everyone agreed that the new recycling center was a wonderful thing for the town of Greenfield. "The more things we recycle and reuse, the fewer natural resources we use up," said Grandfather.

"I know what a natural resource is," announced Benny. "It's trees and land and water."

"That's right," said Henry. "If we use old

paper to make new paper, we save more trees."

"Oh boy," said Benny. "Let's take all our old papers down to the new recycling center today!"

Jessie, Violet, and Henry all liked Benny's idea. After breakfast the four children went into the garage and looked at the piles of recycling. There was a cardboard pile and, next to it, a newspaper pile. There was a box filled with metal cans and a big bag of plastic bottles, too.

"We can ride our bikes," said Henry.

"It's a good thing our bikes all have baskets," said Jessie. "With four bikes, we can take almost half of what's here."

"And then we can take more tomorrow," said Violet.

* * *

"I like the name of this center," said Jessie as they pedaled their bikes through an open gateway. Above their heads was a metal arch with the words "Use It Again Recycling

Center." The entire recycling center was surrounded by a sparkling new chain-link fence.

The Aldens stopped and looked around. Shiny new recycling bins stood in long rows. Each bin was labeled for what went inside. The biggest bin was labeled "Plastic." Off by itself was a huge Dumpster labeled "Other Stuff." Near it was a wooden shed. A young woman lifted an old toaster out of the Other Stuff bin and turned around. As she did so, she saw the children.

"Hello," she said. "Welcome to the new recycling center. I'm Kayla Korty, the manager."

The children introduced themselves.

"You can lean your bikes against a bin," said Kayla, "and I'll give you a tour of the place. But first—what do you think of my collection of treasures?"

The children watched as Kayla put the toaster on a shelf that ran along the outside of the shed. Above the shelf was a handwritten sign: "These May Be Treasures."

The Aldens looked at the things Kayla had on the shelf. Jessie noticed a toaster and a pack of notebooks. Benny noticed two piñatas. Violet noticed a wooden checkerboard without checkers. Henry noticed an old chair that had wooden legs and a wooden back. He could see that the seat of the chair had once been made of woven cane, but that the cane had worn out and broken off. Now there was nothing to sit on.

"I look through the Other Stuff bin each morning," Kayla said. "If anything looks interesting to me, I pull it out and put it here. Feel free to take any of these things home if you want them. There are treasures in recycling," she said with a smile.

"Wow!" said Benny. "Look at that bull piñata! It looks just like the one in Tío's Tacos, my favorite restaurant."

"Oh Benny," laughed Jessie. "You love food so much that every restaurant is your favorite."

Kayla handed the red piñata to Benny. "Would you like to take it home?" she asked.

Benny held the piñata. It was very dusty on top, but he thought he could clean it off. "Yes!" he said. "I'll put it in the sunporch with Mrs. McGregor's frog."

"Frog?" asked Kayla. "You mean that big, green metal frog?"

The children nodded.

"I wish I had never given that frog away," muttered Kayla.

"Why not?" asked Jessie.

"Oh," said Kayla, waving her hand in the air, "just because." She looked at the children. "Benny has a piñata," she said. "Would anybody else like to take a treasure home?"

Neither Henry nor Violet were interested in anything, but Jessie looked at the note-books. "This is a whole pack of notebooks," she said. "And it's unopened."

Kayla shrugged. "Don't ask me why anybody would throw it away," she said. "Would you like it?"

Jessie said she would. She liked to use notebooks to make lists.

"I'll keep the piñata and notebooks here in

my studio until you're ready to leave," Kayla said.

"Your studio?" asked Violet. "Are you an artist?" Violet loved art. Although she was shy, Violet was just as smart as her sister and brothers. All of the Aldens loved puzzles and mysteries.

"Come inside and see," said Kayla. She led the way into the shed. She put Jessie's box of notebooks and Benny's piñata on a table.

The Aldens looked around. They didn't see any paintings. They didn't see any clay.

Henry noticed a table and stool. On the table were small pieces of metal. He saw copper wire and a small soldering iron. "You make jewelry," said Henry.

"Yes!" said Kayla, clapping her hands. She seemed very happy that Henry had guessed what kind of artist she was. "I find small pieces of old metal—like tin, steel, or copper—and I make jewelry out of them."

"You recycle the junk into jewelry," said Jessie with a smile.

"Yes," said Kayla. "Let me show you—"

She was interrupted by a young man standing outside the shed door. He was wearing jeans and a long-sleeved T-shirt.

"Hi Kayla," the young man said. "I'm here to volunteer."

"Oh, hi Ethan," said Kayla. Then she frowned. "I'm so glad you're here. It happened *again* last night."

"Don't worry," said Ethan. "I'll clean it up." He turned and walked away.

"Ethan volunteers to help sort the recycling," Kayla explained.

"I thought people sorted their own recycling once they got here," said Henry.

"Some people don't take the time to sort their recycling once they get here," Kayla explained. "They just dump their bags and boxes and leave. But most people take the time to put their items in the right bins."

"Like we're going to do," said Violet.

Kayla smiled. "Come outside and I'll show you where everything goes."

The four children picked up their recycling bundles and followed Kayla as she showed them around the large recycling center. Except for Kayla's studio, the center was filled with row after row of Dumpsters.

"This center is so new and so clean," said Jessie.

"Yes," said Kayla. She pointed downward. "Notice the new concrete paving," she said. "Most of the center is paved so that when it rains, people don't have to walk through mud."

The Aldens followed Kayla to the first bin.

"Here's where all the cardboard goes," she said, pointing to an extra-large bin.

Henry lifted his large bundle of cardboard and dumped it into the bin.

Next, Kayla showed them where the glass bottles and jars went. "All the glass goes into one of four bins," she said.

"I see," said Jessie. "One is marked *Green*, one is marked Brown, one is marked *Clear*, and the other is marked . . . *Other*."

Kayla laughed. "That's just in case you have glass that's yellow, for example, and you don't know where it goes."

"Or purple," said Violet, who loved the color purple. "I've seen purple glass."

Violet opened a bag they had brought on their bikes and began to drop each glass jar or bottle into the correct bin.

"Let me!" shouted Benny. "I want to drop some bottles."

Violet gave Benny the bag she was holding. It was filled with clear glass bottles and jars. Benny reached in and pulled a bottle out. In order to drop it into the bin for clear glass, Benny had to stand on his tiptoes. Benny dropped each bottle and jar in, one at a time, until the bag was empty.

"Very good, Benny," said Kayla. "All that glass will be melted down and used to make new glass bottles and jars."

Jessie saw that the bin for metal cans was right next to the bins for glass. She opened the bag of metal cans she had brought to the recycling center. At home in their garage, the children had stepped on each metal can in order to crush it. Crushed cans took up less space, so they could fit more in their bag.

Kayla watched as Jessie dropped all the metal cans into the bin.

The Aldens also had two bags of plastic bottles. At home they had crushed these flat, too.

Kayla showed the children where the plastics went. Henry dumped the two bags of plastics into the large bin.

"Now you know where to put cardboard, metal cans, glass jars and bottles, and plastics," said Kayla. "Did you bring any newspapers?" she asked. "Our center collects everything, so you don't have to drive to another town to recycle."

"Yes, we have newspapers, too," said Benny. Kayla showed Benny where to put them. Then he looked past Kayla to where Ethan was working. "What's Ethan doing?" asked Henry.

"He's raking leaves," said Kayla as she walked toward one corner of the recycling center. The children followed.

The children said hello to Ethan and introduced themselves.

"Hi," said Ethan as he kept raking. "Happy to meet you."

"Does your recycling center take leaves?" Jessie asked Kayla.

"It does," said Kayla. People who make their own compost come here and take the leaves and clippings."

"What's compost?" asked Benny.

Jessie had learned about compost in school. She explained to Benny that compost is made of plants or plant parts that have decayed. Compost might also contain eggshells or coffee grounds. "The decayed parts are mixed into dirt to make it richer," she explained. "Richer dirt helps grow better crops."

Benny knew what crops were. They were plant foods like tomatoes, corn, and carrots. Benny loved all foods.

Violet didn't understand why the leaves and grass clippings weren't inside plastic bags already. She wondered why Ethan had to rake them up. "Did somebody throw their leaves all over the ground?" she asked Kayla.

Kayla frowned. "No," she said. "People stuff their leaves and grass into plastic bags and drop them off here. But it seems that somebody is breaking into the center and then breaking open all the bags of leaves and grass."

"That's terrible," said Violet. "Why would anybody do something mean like that?"

Ethan raked so close to where Violet was standing that she had to jump away.

"I don't know," said Kayla. "But thankfully Ethan has volunteered to clean up the mess. I don't know what I'd do without him."

"Do you need more volunteers at the recycling center?" asked Henry.

"I sure do!" said Kayla. "You see those boxes and bags?" she asked, pointing to a large stack near the front gate. "I need volunteers to open those up and sort them into the proper bins."

The Aldens looked at one another. "We would like to volunteer," said Jessie.

Kayla looked at them. "Really?" she asked. The four children nodded.

"Thank you," said Kayla. "Thank you so much."

"Ethan," asked Kayla, "would you like one of the Aldens to help you rake up the leaves and grass?"

"No!" shouted Ethan. "I need to do this myself."

Kayla stepped back. She seemed surprised by Ethan's sudden answer. "Well, okay," she said.

"Henry, Jessie, Violet, and Benny, please wait for me by the front gate, right by that huge pile of stuff," Kayla said. "I'll bring you each a pair of gloves."

The children walked to the front gate and looked at the bags and boxes, each one filled with recyclables.

They noticed a woman standing on the sidewalk across the street. She had her arms folded across her chest. She was staring at them with an angry look on her face.

CHAPTER 2

Another Break-in

The next morning the children loaded their bikes with more recycling and pedaled to the Use It Again Recycling Center. Even though they had worked hard yesterday, they had enjoyed it. Helping other people felt good. And helping people recycle felt especially good.

When the Aldens arrived at the center, they saw more boxes and bags of trash on the sidewalk along the outside of the recycling center.

"Wow!" said Benny. "We worked hard yesterday, and now there are new bags and boxes to sort. There are more bags and boxes today than there were yesterday!"

Henry laughed. "That's good," he said. "It means that people are really using the recycling center."

The Alden children expected to see Kayla sorting through the bin marked "Other Stuff," looking for what she called "treasures" and putting them on the shelf outside her shed. Violet in particular was hoping to find something purple to take home and reuse.

What they found instead was a big mess. The large Other Stuff bin lay on its side on the concrete. Things that had been placed inside the bin lay scattered all over the concrete. A man wearing a golf cap, a long-sleeved shirt, green pants, and hiking boots was bent over, picking things up off the ground and throwing them back down on the concrete. Kayla was trying to talk to him, but the man wasn't paying any attention.

Quickly, the children leaned their bikes against a bin.

"What happened?" Henry asked Kayla.

"There was another break-in last night," Kayla answered. "This time the person tipped over my Other Stuff Dumpster."

Henry looked at the Dumpster, which lay on its side. Then he looked at the fence behind the Dumpster. The top part of the chain-link fence was bent inward. *Whoever did this climbed the new fence*, thought Henry.

Jessie was looking at the Dumpster, too. "If we all help, do you think we can tip the Dumpster back up?" she asked Kayla.

"That's a good idea," said Kayla. "Chad, do you think you can help us?" she asked the man in the golf cap.

The man didn't answer. He kept picking up and putting down all the things that had been in the Dumpster.

Kayla spoke more loudly. "Chad? Can you help us?"

"What?" he asked, straightening up.

"Can you help us turn this Dumpster

upright, the way it should be?" Kayla asked.

Chad frowned. "Yeah," he said. "Okay."

The Aldens and Kayla and Chad all worked together to tip the Dumpster upright.

"Thank you," said Kayla. "You kids have been so helpful!"

"And we can help today, too," said Benny.

Henry spoke to the man in the golf cap. "We're the Aldens," he said. "I'm Henry, and these are my sisters, Jessie and Violet, and my brother, Benny."

The man frowned. "I've read about you Aldens in the newspaper. You're the kids who think you can solve mysteries," he sneered. "Ha!"

"We know we can solve mysteries," said Jessie. "You didn't tell us your name."

The man glared at Jessie. "Chad Foster," he grunted. Then he bent back down and began scooping things up and dumping them into the bin.

"Are you a volunteer?" Jessie asked him.

"Yeah. And I don't have time to chat," he said.

Jessie thought Chad Foster was a very unfriendly man.

Kayla looked at the Aldens and shrugged her shoulders, as if to say she didn't know what Chad's problem was.

"I'm so glad you're here," she said to the children. "May I split you up into two work groups?"

"Sure," said Henry.

Kayla smiled. "Okay. Jessie and Benny, I'd like you to help Chad pick everything up and toss it back into the Dumpster."

"No!" shouted Chad, straightening up again. "I don't need a bunch of kids around while I'm trying to work."

Kayla walked up to Chad. "I expect everybody who volunteers here to treat one another with courtesy. If you can't do that, Chad, then you should leave right now."

Jessie thought that Chad looked shocked by what Kayla had said. He blinked twice, then looked at her and Benny.

"Yeah," he said at last. "All right. They can help."

"Good," said Kayla.

She smiled at Jessie and Benny. "After I show Henry and Violet what I'd like them to do, I'll come back and see how you're doing."

As Jessie and Benny began to pick up the scattered trash, Kayla took Violet and Henry back toward the entrance to Use It Again. She led them past the gate to the lawn. The large pile of bags and boxes that the children had seen when they arrived were scattered on the lawn and against the curb.

"Usually I haul these in every morning as soon as I arrive," Kayla said. "But this morning the first thing I saw was the overturned Dumpster. I stood there looking at it, and then this man—Chad—came in and said he'd like to help."

Kayla looked over her shoulder to where Chad, Jessie, and Benny were working. "I wish he were more friendly, but the center needs all the help it can get. Somebody doesn't want the recycling center to be here." As Kayla said this, she turned and looked across the street.

Henry and Violet turned to see where Kayla was staring. They saw a woman standing on the sidewalk across the street. It was the same woman they had seen standing there yesterday. She was wearing bright red rubber boots, corduroy pants, and a jacket. Her hair was white. In one hand she held a small garden trowel. In the other she held a plastic bottle.

Violet noticed that Kayla frowned at the woman, and that the woman frowned back at Kayla. Then the woman crossed the street and walked right up to them.

"It's past ten o'clock in the morning," the woman shouted. "And your trash is still on the public sidewalk!"

As she spoke, the woman shook her plastic bottle at Kayla.

Violet noticed that it was a bottle of Doo-Dah Tea with a red label. Sometimes Violet drank Doo-Dah Tea. She knew that the red label meant the tea was raspberry flavored.

"Mrs. Wickett, I'm sorry about this," said

Kayla. "Ever since you complained, I've been coming to work early just to move everything inside."

"Well, then why is the trash still there?" demanded Mrs. Wickett. Henry could see that she was very angry.

Without waiting for an answer, Mrs. Wickett continued. "I'm going to report you to the mayor's office," she said. "I'm going to get this center closed down."

"Somebody has been breaking into the center and tearing open bags of trash," said Kayla. "And tipping over Dumpsters." Now Kayla was angry, too. "I think you're the one who's breaking into the center," she said. "You're the one who's against recycling!"

"What?!" shouted Mrs. Wickett. "Me, break into a recycling center? Don't be ridiculous."

Henry watched as Mrs. Wickett unscrewed the top of her bottle and drank the rest of her raspberry tea. She screwed the top back on, then she carefully placed the bottle inside one of the open boxes. Henry noticed that the box she placed it in held other plastic bottles.

"Recycling is a good thing," Mrs. Wickett told Kayla. "But leaving trash on public sidewalks is a *bad* thing. Look at this," she said, kicking a cardboard box. "When the center is closed, people leave their recycling outside the fence. When I leave for work each evening, all I see are bags of trash! When I come home at midnight, all I see are boxes of junk!"

"But I explained—" Kayla started to say.

"No!" shouted Mrs. Wickett. "I'm going to call the mayor's office and complain!"

Henry and Violet watched Mrs. Wickett stomp across the street and into her own backyard.

"Wow," said Henry. "Mrs. Wickett is one very upset person."

Violet looked at all the bags and boxes. "I can see why she's upset," said Violet softly. "There's a lot of trash here."

"We'll take it all inside and start to sort it," Henry told Kayla. "But Violet is right,

Kayla. Isn't there any way you could keep the recycling center open until midnight so people can take their trash inside?"

"No," said Kayla firmly. "If I left the center open that late, somebody could break into my studio."

Kayla picked up two bags and carried them inside. Henry picked up a large box, and Violet picked up a smaller box.

"I think Mrs. Wickett is the person who's breaking into the center," said Kayla as the three of them worked.

"If she is, we'll find out," said Violet. "We will help you."

Kayla stopped to look at Violet and Henry. "You will?" she asked.

"Yes," said Henry. "We volunteer to help you sort recycled things, and we also volunteer to help find out who's breaking into the center."

Suddenly Kayla smiled. "Okay," she said. "You just might be the best volunteers ever!"

CHAPTER 3

Treasures from Scrap

Jessie and Benny helped Chad pick up everything that had been dumped out of the Other Stuff bin. During the whole time they had helped, Chad had not spoken to them at all. Jessie noticed that each time she or Benny put something into the bin, Chad walked over and looked into the bin.

Why is he looking at each thing we do? she wondered.

Just as the three of them finished, Kayla arrived.

28

She smiled. "Thank you. This looks neat and clean," she said.

"Where's the rest of it?" asked Chad.

Kayla looked confused. "The rest of what?" she asked.

"The rest of what goes in this Other Stuff bin," he said.

"Oh," said Kayla. "This is everything. There isn't any more."

Chad shook his head. "There's got to be more. You must have a second bin marked Other Stuff."

"No," said Kayla. "We don't. But you can help Jessie and Benny sort all the dropped-off bags and boxes into the right bins."

Kayla pointed to a stack of dropped-off recycling.

"I can show you how," Benny said to Chad. "We did the same thing yesterday."

Chad ignored Benny. "What happens to the things in the Other Stuff bin?" he asked Kayla. "Where do they go?"

"Well," said Kayla, "each morning I look through the bin and take out anything that looks like somebody might want it. I put it on the shelf that runs along the shed. Or underneath the shelf, if it doesn't fit." Kayla pointed to the shed.

Jessie noticed that all the things that had been on the shelf and under it yesterday were gone. The shelf was empty.

Chad looked toward the shelf. "Then what?" he asked.

"When people drop off their recycling, some of them look at what I have out there. Sometimes people take things home and reuse them. Yesterday, for example, I had an old caned chair out there. Somebody took it home with them," said Kayla with a smile. "I'll bet they're going to weave new cane into the seat, and then they'll clean the chair and refinish it. Then they'll use it for years and years. Isn't that wonderful?" she asked.

"I think so," said Jessie.

"Yes," said Benny. "Henry can fix things and make them work. He fixed my bike."

Chad stared at Benny. "Did your brother take the old chair?" he asked.

"No," said Benny, "but we saw it yesterday when we were here."

Chad looked at the shelf, then at the bin, then at Kayla. "What happens when this bin gets full?" he asked.

"Trucks come twice a week," Kayla explained. "Every Wednesday they take the glass, plastics, and newspapers. Every Saturday they take more glass, plastics, and newspapers. On Saturday they also take the cardboard and everything from the Other Stuff bin."

"You're very interested in recycling," Jessie said to Chad.

He frowned. "I guess I am," he said. Then Chad turned to Kayla again. "Where do the trucks take the bins?" he asked.

"To a recycling plant in Watertown," said Kayla as she turned to pick up a box of glass jars. "Benny and Jessie, can you show Chad how to sort the recycling?"

Jessie took the box from Kayla. "Sure," she said. "The glass bins are over here," she told Chad.

But Chad just stood there.

Kayla went back to work in her shed. Jessie and Benny began dropping the bottles and jars into the correct bins.

Benny stood on his tiptoes and looked into the bin for brown glass. Still, he could barely see over the top.

Jessie laughed. "Here's a wooden box to stand on," she said. She turned the box over and put it down near Benny.

"I see a plastic bottle," said Benny. "It doesn't belong with glass."

Benny stood on his tiptoes on the wooden box, but he still wasn't tall enough to reach inside the bin.

"Here," said Jessie, "I can reach it."

She reached into the bin for brown glass and pulled out a plastic bottle. The green label read Doo-Dah Tea. Benny knew that the green label meant the tea was mint flavored. Benny took the bottle from Jessie and walked over to the plastics bin. He threw the bottle into the bin.

"The bottle was in the wrong place," Benny

said to Chad. "Somebody threw plastic into the Dumpster for brown glass."

Chad suddenly looked interested. "What?" he asked. "What did you just say?"

Benny repeated what he had said.

"Hmmm," said Chad. "That could be it. It could be in the wrong place."

"*What* could be in the wrong place?" Jessie asked.

"Hmmm," said Chad again. He didn't say anything else.

"Are you ready to help recycle now?" Benny asked.

"No," snapped Chad. "I have something else to do."

Jessie and Benny watched Chad walk away. He didn't say good-bye to them. He didn't say good-bye to Violet or Henry, either, when he walked past where they were working.

"What a grump," said Jessie.

"Maybe he's just hungry," said Benny.

Jessie laughed. "Oh Benny," she said. "I don't need a watch when you're around, do I?"

"Why not?" asked her brother.

"Because when you're hungry in the middle of the day, I know it's time for lunch."

The children finished sorting recycled materials and rode their bikes home along the bike path.

As they were pedaling, Violet heard footsteps behind them. She could tell they were the footsteps of somebody running very fast.

Before Violet could even turn around to see who was running, she heard somebody say, "Hi Benny! Hi Violet! Hi Jessie and Henry!"

It was Ethan. He waved his hand as he raced past them.

Violet saw that today Ethan was wearing shorts and a tank top.

"Ethan sure can run fast," said Benny as he pedaled his bike.

"Yes," said Jessie. "I'll bet he runs track. That looked like a track uniform he was wearing."

* * *

When they arrived back home, the children propped their bikes against the garage and walked into the sunporch. Benny patted the big green frog and looked up at his bull piñata, which Henry had hung from the sunporch ceiling.

Mrs. McGregor was in the kitchen, reading the newspaper and drinking a bottle of tea.

Jessie noticed that the bottle had a green label. It was mint-flavored Doo-Dah Tea.

"What's in the news?" Jessie asked Mrs. McGregor.

"What's for lunch?" asked Benny at the same time.

Everybody laughed.

"I'll answer both questions after you all wash the recycling dirt off your hands and sit down. I've already set the table."

After the children had washed, Mrs. McGregor brought out a plate full of vegetables and another plate full of kebabs—small pieces of chicken on skewers. Finally, she gave each of the children a bowl of dipping sauce.

"Chicken!" said Benny. "I love chicken." He dipped a carrot into the sauce. "I love carrots, too."

"This is so good," said Violet. "Thank you, Mrs. McGregor."

Mrs. McGregor smiled. "You're welcome," she said.

"So," said Jessie, pointing to the newspaper Mrs. McGregor had been reading, "what's in the news?" All the Aldens loved to read and get information, but Jessie loved it the best.

"Well," answered Mrs. McGregor, "the police still haven't caught the person who robbed Jonah's Jewelry Store a few weeks ago. Somebody broke into the store around midnight, stole a bag of diamonds, and got away before the police arrived."

"Did the store have a burglar alarm?" asked Henry.

"Yes," said Mrs. McGregor, "but the thief must have moved very quickly—just like Benny is moving for more chicken!"

Indeed, Benny was in the middle of piling more kebabs onto his plate.

"If there's food around, Benny will eat it," Henry kidded.

Then Henry also reached for more chicken. So did Jessie and so did Violet.

"Maybe the thief was Ethan," said Benny. "Ethan moves very, very fast!"

Jessie explained to Mrs. McGregor who Ethan was.

"So," asked Mrs. McGregor, "what will you children be doing the rest of the afternoon?"

"We're going back to the recycling center," said Violet. "We have a mystery to solve."

"A mystery?" asked Mrs. McGregor. "What kind of mystery can there be at a recycling center?"

"Somebody is breaking in at night and opening bags of leaves," Benny explained. He stopped eating long enough to make a big circle with his arms, to show how big the bags of leaves were. "And they tipped over a big Dumpster, too," he added. "The one your frog came from."

"And my notebooks," said Jessie.

"And Benny's piñata," said Henry.

* * *

After the children had eaten lunch and helped Mrs. McGregor with the dishes, they pedaled back to the recycling center. Everything at the center looked neat and clean. All the bins were lined up, and except for the bags of leaves and grass in the corner, all the trash was off the ground.

"Mrs. Wickett should be happy with how neat this looks," said Violet.

"Yes, but we worked all morning to help sort the bags and boxes," said Henry. "After the center closes, people start leaving more boxes and bags out on the sidewalk. That's what gets Mrs. Wickett upset."

Jessie and Benny hadn't met Mrs. Wickett, but Henry and Violet told them what had happened earlier that morning.

"I wonder why Kayla won't leave the center open at night," Jessie said. "That way people could bring their recycling inside."

"She said she doesn't want people going into her studio," said Violet.

The center was very quiet. The children went to see if Kayla was in her studio.

The door was open and Kayla was inside, reading the newspaper.

"Oh, hi," Kayla said when she heard them. She stood up quickly and spread the open newspaper across the top of a bench.

Jessie noticed that Kayla had placed the newspaper on top of something sparkly.

"I didn't expect you again until tomorrow morning," Kayla said.

Jessie noticed that the page Kayla had been reading showed a picture of Jonah's Jewelry Store. *She's reading the same article that Mrs. McGregor was reading*, thought Jessie. *The one about the stolen diamonds.*

"We can sort more recycling," said Henry. "And we promised we would find out who's breaking into the center."

"Oh." Kayla frowned. "Well," she said, "there's no more sorting to do this afternoon." She glanced at the newspaper she had spread across the bench. "I'm very happy with the work you did," she told the children. "Ethan didn't come in this morning, so I really needed the four of you."

"We saw Ethan today," said Benny. "He was running."

"Yes," said Kayla with a smile. "Ethan runs track and jumps hurdles. He goes to college on a track scholarship. He's always training."

Suddenly Kayla clapped her hands. "You know what?" she asked the Aldens. "If you want, I can show you how I make jewelry from scrap. It's my own little way of recycling."

"Yes, please," said Violet. "I would love to see."

Her brothers and sister were also interested in seeing how Kayla made jewelry from scrap.

"As you can see, my work space is very small," said Kayla. "But I'm very organized." She pointed to one end of her workbench. "That's where I keep tin cans. I make pins and earrings from them. I also make mobiles, like that one." She pointed to a mobile of five colorful airplanes. "Each of those planes is made from a tin can."

"Wow!" said Benny. "I like it!"

Kayla smiled. "This pile contains small pieces of brass, copper, silver, and gold. You'd be surprised how much metal is thrown away. I use the small pieces to make rings or bracelets or key rings."

"These are beautiful," said Violet, looking at some rings.

"Where do you sell your jewelry?" asked Henry as he looked at a key ring. "You don't have any signs outside that tell people you sell jewelry. How will they know about it?"

Kayla frowned. "I wanted Jonah's Jewelry Store to sell my rings and bracelets and pins," she said, "but Mr. Jonah called them junk. All he cares about are diamonds."

Then Kayla looked at Henry. "You've given me an idea," she said. "I should put a sign on the outside of this shed. Maybe it should say 'Recycled Jewelry,' or something like that." Kayla seemed lost in thought.

Benny saw the sparkly thing under the edge of the newspaper that Kayla had put on the bench. "What's that?" he asked, pointing. "Is it a diamond?"

Kayla pulled the piece from underneath the newspaper.

Jessie noticed that Kayla pressed the newspaper down around whatever else it was covering.

"This is a key ring," said Kayla, handing it to Benny. "The sparkling thing is just a piece of glass I found and polished."

"It looks just like a diamond!" said Benny.

Kayla laughed. "Yes, it does," she said.

Henry asked if he could see the key ring, and Benny gave it to him. "This is cool," said Henry. "May I buy it?"

"Oh, I don't know," Kayla mumbled.

"I really like it," said Henry. He held the square of metal in his hand. He liked the way the piece of glass was set in the center. He saw that Kayla had drilled a hole into one end of the metal and put a key ring through the hole.

Finally, Kayla told Henry how much she wanted for the key ring.

Henry paid her. Then he put his keys on the new key ring and put the key ring on his belt.

"Well," said Kayla, "Jessie has notebooks,

Benny has a piñata, and Henry has a key ring. Every Alden except Violet has something from the recycling center."

Kayla looked at Violet. "Have you seen anything you would like?" she asked.

Violet smiled shyly. "I'm still looking for something purple," she said.

CHAPTER 4

Tamales and Tea

That evening Grandfather and the children went out to Tío's Tacos for dinner.

Grandfather parked the car, and the five of them walked two blocks to the restaurant.

"Look," said Jessie as they neared the restaurant. "There's Jonah's Jewelry Store. It's right across the street from Tío's Tacos."

"I didn't know you were interested in jewelry," Grandfather said to Jessie, who was already looking at the jewelry in Jonah's window.

"I'm interested that Jonah's Jewelry Store got robbed a few weeks ago," Jessie explained. "I never noticed the store before."

Violet and Henry and Benny looked in the window, also.

"I like Kayla's jewelry better," said Violet.

"Me too," said Henry. "And it's recycled."

"I like Tío's Tacos," said Benny, looking across the street at the restaurant.

"Okay, okay," Grandfather said with a laugh. "Let's all cross the street."

After they crossed the street, Benny stopped in front of the door to Tío's Tacos. Even though the Alden family visited Tío's Tacos often, Benny sometimes didn't pay attention to signs. This time he noticed a sign in the window. Because Benny was just learning to read, he wanted to read it. "Open," he read. "Until. One a.m." Benny frowned. "What does *a.m.* mean?" he asked.

"That means that Tío's Tacos is open very late," explained Grandfather.

"One a.m. is one hour past midnight," said Henry.

Benny's eyes opened wide. "Do people eat that late?" he asked.

"Some people do," said Grandfather. "People who work in places that close at ten o'clock or eleven o'clock might want to eat after they leave work."

"*Sí*, that is correct," said Tío as he came to their table. His real name was Miguel, but he insisted that his customers call him Tío, which means *uncle* in Spanish.

Tío shook hands with Grandfather and each of the children, calling them by name. "I could not help but overhear what you were saying," he explained. "People who work the evening hours, they need a place to eat after work. The people who work in the jewelry store, for example. Their store closes at nine o'clock. Tío's Tacos is open, and those good people come here to eat good food."

"We're here to eat good food, too," said Benny.

Tío smiled at Benny. "Yes," he said. "You and your family come here often. I am glad to see you again."

"I'm happy to hear that your business is good," Grandfather said. "That makes it worth staying open so late."

Tío scratched his chin. "It is good, but it is slow after midnight. Only Mrs. Wickett comes in, and sometimes the man who used to work at the jewelry store." Tío seemed lost in thought. "It would be good if three or four more people came in after midnight."

"Look!" said Benny suddenly, pointing toward the ceiling. "You have new piñatas!"

Everybody looked upward, where five new piñatas were hanging from the ceiling.

"You have two fish, a star, a llama, and a donkey," said Benny.

"You are a very observant *niño*," Tio said. "And do you know *why* I have new piñatas?" he asked.

Benny shook his head. Tío looked to the other children.

"New piñatas are pretty," said Violet. "Their colors are very bright."

"That is it exactly!" said Tío, beaming with pleasure. "The old piñatas, they became dusty on top. And their colors faded from the sun. So I bought new ones."

"The new ones are beautiful," said Violet.

Jessie and Henry and Grandfather all agreed.

"I am happy to hear that you like my new decorations," said Tío. "I changed them a few days ago, and that made one customer very angry."

"Why was that?" asked Henry.

Tío shrugged. "Who knows. He said he liked the old ones and didn't like the new ones."

"Are the piñatas filled with prizes?" Benny asked. "Games and cookies and candy?" he added.

Tío smiled. "That is a secret."

"Why is it a secret?" Benny asked.

"Because if I told you the piñatas were filled with something, I think you would want to break one open just to see."

Benny looked at the piñatas. He thought it would be fun to break one open. He was going to say something, but just then many customers came in at once, and Tío had to seat them.

Violet looked at the people who had come into the restaurant. One of the people was Ethan, who was still wearing running shorts and a tank top.

"Look," said Violet to her sister and brothers. "I wonder if Ethan is going to eat here."

Jessie, Henry, and Benny all watched Ethan.

"Who's Ethan?" asked Grandfather.

Henry explained that Ethan was a volunteer at the recycling center.

"Ethan is buying two bottles of Doo-Dah Tea from the front of the store," said Benny.

"Mint-flavored Doo-Dah Tea," said Violet, who could see that both labels were green.

The children watched as Ethan paid for his tea, said goodbye to Tío, and left.

A server came to take their dinner orders. As they waited for their food, the children and Grandfather talked.

"I'll bet my bull piñata used to be in Tío's

restaurant," said Benny. "I'll bet Tío took it to the recycling center and Kayla found it in the Other Stuff bin and then I took it home. When we get home I'm going to break it open and see what's inside!"

"Well," said Grandfather, "it's your piñata and you may break it open if you want to. But usually people save piñatas for special occasions."

"Yes," said Jessie, "like a birthday."

"Or a party with friends," said Henry.

"Can we have a party soon?" asked Benny.

The children talked about whether or not to have a party, but they never reached a decision. Their food arrived, and soon they forgot about everything except the delicious tacos, tamales, and beans and rice.

As they were finishing their meal, Henry looked up as the restaurant door opened. He saw Mrs. Wickett walk in. She was dressed up. Henry saw a sparkling pin on her blouse.

She spoke to Tío, who was at the cash register. Tío turned to the cooler alongside the wall, opened it, and took out six bottles of Doo-Dah Tea. Henry noticed that all bottles had red labels. *Mrs. Wickett sure likes raspberry-flavored tea*, thought Henry. He watched as she paid for the tea and Tío put the plastic bottles into a paper bag.

As she turned to go, Mrs. Wickett looked toward the Aldens' table. She stared for a minute, then walked over to them.

"Hello," she said to Henry and Violet. "Didn't I see you this morning outside the recycling center?"

"Yes," said Henry. He introduced Grandfather, Jessie, Violet, Benny, and himself to Mrs. Wickett.

"Tío told us that you're a good customer of his," said Grandfather.

"Yes," she answered. "Tío serves wonderful food. When I leave work, the first thing I smell is the wonderful aroma from Tío's Tacos. So naturally, I come here." Mrs. Wickett patted the bag she was holding. "And Tío always has my favorite tea on hand."

"You must work at Jonah's Jewelry Store," said Grandfather with a smile.

Mrs. Wickett looked surprised. "Why, yes," she said, "but how did you know that?"

"Oh," said Grandfather, "I've learned a few detective skills from my grandchildren."

Mrs. Wickett looked confused.

"Jonah's Jewelry Store is the only store that's open late in this two-block area," Grandfather explained.

"Ahhh!" said Mrs. Wickett. "Very good. I'm their bookkeeper. I could work days, but I prefer to work nights. Everything is quiet then so I can concentrate on the numbers. Well, it's so nice to have met you, but I must get back to work."

The Aldens said good-bye to Mrs. Wickett and watched her walk out the door and down the block.

"Did you notice the jewelry she was wearing?" Violet asked. "She had a diamond pin on her blouse and three diamond rings on her fingers."

Grandfather smiled at Violet. "You make it sound suspicious," he said. "But Mrs. Wickett works at a jewelry store. Maybe she's supposed to wear jewelry while she works there."

"Or maybe she can buy it because the store gives her a big discount," said Jessie.

"Or maybe she's not wearing diamonds," said Henry. "Maybe she's wearing glass that looks like diamonds."

CHAPTER 5

Footprints and Key Rings

The next morning, the children loaded Grandfather's car with recyclables, and he drove them to the recycling center. They unloaded the recyclables into the proper bins and said good-bye to Grandfather.

"Let's walk around the outside of the recycling center," said Henry.

"Good idea," said Jessie. "We might find footprints."

The children walked out the front gate of the recycling center and turned right to follow the chain-link fence around the outside of the center.

Violet noticed that Mrs. Wickett was sitting on her porch, holding something in her lap. Violet waved. Mrs. Wickett waved back.

There weren't any suspicious-looking footprints along the front of the recycling center. There were none along the side.

But as soon as the children turned the second corner, Henry raised his hand.

"Stop!" he said.

Benny, Violet, and Jessie crowded around Henry so they could see what he was looking at.

On the ground were two blurred footprints. The toes of the footprints were clearer than the rest of the footprints. The toes were pointing toward the back fence of the recycling center.

"Look," said Benny, pointing through the fence. "The toes point right at the bags filled with leaves and grass on the other side of the fence."

Jessie stared at the two prints. "The back footprint is a left foot," she said. "And the front footprint is a right foot."

"The two footprints are very far apart," said Violet. "It looks like somebody was running."

"We don't have our camera with us," said Jessie. Then she grinned. "But I do have one of my recycled notebooks!"

Henry pulled a small tape measure out of his pocket. Henry loved tools, and he often had some with him. He measured one of the footprints from front to back. "Exactly eleven inches," he said.

Jessie wrote that in her notebook. Then she sketched the tread pattern of the shoe.

When Jessie's sketch was finished, the children bent down to hold the drawing near the footprint.

"Good work," Henry told his sister. "Now look at the top of the fence," he said.

Jessie and Violet looked. "The top of the fence is fine," said Jessie. "It's not bent at all."

"That's right," said Henry. He looked up

at the sky. "It looks like it's going to rain, so it's a good thing we have this drawing."

"Yes," said Benny, "because the rain will wash everything away."

Being careful not to step on the two footprints, the Aldens continued walking along the back of the recycling center.

Soon Henry raised his hand again and said, "Stop!"

"Wow," said Benny. "More footprints! Look at them! They're all on top of one another."

"Hmmm," said Jessie. She was looking through the chain-link fence into the recycling center. The footprints were opposite the Other Stuff bin that had been tipped over yesterday.

"I think we can draw some conclusions," said Jessie. "First, these footprints were made by a different person. They don't match the first set."

"Maybe," said Henry. "Or maybe they were made by the same person, but the person was wearing different shoes," said

Henry. "There's one way to find out."

Henry pulled the small tape measure out of his pocket again. It took him a while to find a whole footprint. When he did, he measured it. "These footprints are only nine-and-a-half inches long," he said. "They were made by a different person."

Jessie wrote the information on another page of her notebook. "There's something very different about these footprints," she said. "Instead of being far apart like the other set, these ones are close together."

"They're all on top of one another," Benny reminded her. "See," he said, pointing to where one heel mark was pressed deeply into another toe mark.

Henry stood and examined the top of the chain-link fence. It still had the same damage he had seen the first day. "The fence is bent inward here," he said.

"So somebody climbed the fence here," said Jessie.

"And whoever it was kept slipping off," Violet said. "Whoever it was kept falling back to the ground onto his own footprints!"

"Or *her* own footprints," said Jessie.

Jessie drew the tread mark of a toe and of a heel. Everybody looked at her drawing and back at the fence.

"You know what this means," Jessie said.

Henry nodded. "It means we have two different people breaking into the recycling center."

"One wears a shoe that's eleven inches long," said Jessie. "And the other wears a shoe that's nine-and-a-half inches long."

"Are the two people working together?" asked Benny.

"I don't think so," said Henry. "And I think each of them is breaking into the recycling center for a different reason."

"Two people, two reasons," said Jessie. "That makes sense to me."

The children talked about their discovery as they walked around the last side of the recycling center. When they turned the final corner, they saw Mrs. Wickett leaning over one of the boxes people had left outside the center. She was wearing her bright red rubber boots.

"We're about to take all those bags and boxes inside," Henry told her.

Benny walked up to the box Mrs. Wickett had been bending over. A bottle of raspberry Doo-Dah Tea lay on top of the box. Benny thought that Mrs. Wickett must have put it there.

Mrs. Wickett didn't say anything. She just stood there holding a brown paper bag.

"Is something wrong?" Violet asked her.

Mrs. Wickett let out a long sigh. "Yes," she said at last, "something is wrong."

The children waited. "What is it?" Violet asked at last.

Mrs. Wickett looked at the children. "I behaved badly yesterday morning. Violet and Henry, I'm sorry that I was rude to you. Will you accept my apology?"

Violet and Henry said yes.

"I was rude to Kayla, too," said Mrs. Wickett, staring into the recycling center.

When it looked as if Mrs. Wickett might

stand there forever, Jessie spoke. "You would probably feel better if you apologized to Kayla," she said.

"Will you go in with me?" Mrs. Wickett asked them.

The Aldens walked into the recycling center with Mrs. Wickett. As soon as they entered, they heard Kayla shouting.

The four children and Mrs. Wickett walked toward the main recycling bins. There was Chad, pulling plastics and glass out of the bins and throwing them on the ground again.

"Stop! Stop!" Kayla shouted at Chad. "You're supposed to put things into the bins, not take them out!"

Chad stuck his head into the plastics bin and said something.

"I can't hear you!" Kayla said.

Chad pulled his head out. "I said I lost something yesterday and I want to find it."

Then Chad seemed to notice the Aldens and Mrs. Wickett.

"What are *you* doing here?" Chad asked Mrs. Wickett.

"Hello Chad," she answered. "I'm here because I live across the street. You haven't been in to work since the jewel robbery. What happened?"

"I quit," he said. "I don't want to work at a place that gets robbed."

"Oh," said Mrs. Wickett.

"What did you do at Jonah's Jewelry Store?" Henry asked Chad.

Chad started to answer, then stopped. "I sold jewelry to customers," he said finally. As Chad answered, he kept looking into the glass bins and moving things around.

"You're making me nervous doing that," Kayla told him. "If you tell me what you lost, I'll help you find it."

"I can help, too," said Benny.

Chad looked at everybody looking at him. "Uh," he said, "I lost a pocket watch."

"We'll help you find it," said Jessie.

"I never saw you with a pocket watch," said Mrs. Wickett.

Chad frowned. "I don't want anybody's help. Just leave me alone!" He turned back to the bins and kept on searching.

Mrs. Wickett cleared her throat. "Kayla," she said, "I owe you an apology. Even though you shouldn't allow people to leave their trash on the outside of the fence, I shouldn't have shouted at you. I'm sorry."

Kayla seemed to think about the apology. "That's okay," she finally replied. "We all have bad days."

Mrs. Wickett opened the brown paper bag she had been holding. "I brought some bottled tea as a peace offering," she said. "Would you like some? It's cold and refreshing."

"Sure," said Kayla with a smile. She accepted a bottle of raspberry Doo-Dah Tea.

Next, Mrs. Wickett offered each of the children a bottle of tea. All of the bottles had red labels.

Violet and Benny said no, thank you. Henry and Jessie each took a bottle of tea and thanked Mrs. Wickett.

"Chad," said Mrs. Wickett, "I didn't know you would be here, or I would have brought mint-flavored tea, too. I know it's your favorite. Would you like a raspberry Doo-Dah Tea?"

"No, thanks," said Chad. He stood with his back to the Dumpster for clear glass.

Henry thought Chad looked as if he was waiting for everybody to leave.

"Hey!" said Chad suddenly, pointing at Henry's key ring. "What's that?"

Henry lifted his key ring upward. "It's my new key ring," he said. "I bought it from Kayla yesterday."

"I have more if you're interested," Kayla told Chad.

"Is that a diamond inset?" asked Chad. "On a piece of scrap metal?"

"No," said Kayla. "It's not a diamond, it's glass. And I happen to like jewelry made from scrap metal."

"Let me see it," said Chad, holding his hand out to Henry.

Henry thought Chad had very bad manners. He demanded the key ring instead of asking, and he didn't even say "please."

Henry took the key ring off his belt and handed it to Chad.

And then, to Henry's surprise, and perhaps to everybody's surprise, Chad took a small magnifying glass out of his pocket. Using the magnifying glass, Chad studied the sparkling stone set in the middle of the key ring. Henry knew that jewelers used such magnifying glasses to look at precious stones more closely. Watchmakers used them, too. Henry just couldn't remember what the small tool was called.

"Yep," said Chad. "It's glass." He folded up his tiny magnifying glass and handed the key ring back to Henry.

"I'm surprised to see you carrying a loupe around," Mrs. Wickett said to Chad. "If I'm not mistaken, I saw the name *Jonah's Jewelry Store* on that loupe."

That's what it's called, thought Henry. *A loupe*.

"So what?" challenged Chad. "I took a little something with me as a souvenir."

Chad steals things, thought Violet. *He took*

the loupe from Jonah's Jewelry Store.

"May I see your key ring?" Mrs. Wickett asked Henry.

"Sure," he said, handing it to her.

Mrs. Wickett looked at the key ring closely. "Hmmm," she said, handing it back to Henry. "Very nice work," she said to Kayla.

"Thank you," said Kayla.

Violet could tell that the praise made Kayla happy.

"All my jewelry is very affordable because I make it out of old metal and glass—things I find in these recycling bins. I like to tell people that there are treasures in recycling. Not just in reusing all our plastic and glass and paper again, but in reusing everything."

"Jessie and I each took a treasure home from the Other Stuff bin," said Benny proudly. "And after we each took something home, somebody else took an old chair home."

"Really?" asked Chad, looking at Benny. "What day was that?"

"It was Monday," said Jessie.

When Chad didn't say anything, Jessie

asked him if Monday was the day he lost something.

"I'm not sure," said Chad. "I'm just not sure." Then he turned his back to them all and walked down the row of Dumpsters.

Mrs. Wickett turned to Kayla. "I would like to buy a piece of your inexpensive jewelry," she said.

"Oh good!" said Kayla. "Let me show you what I have."

The children watched as Kayla and Mrs. Wickett headed for the shed that was Kayla's studio. The last thing they heard was Mrs. Wickett saying that something had to be done about all the recycling left alongside the public sidewalk each night.

"Something has to be done about it right now," said Jessie.

"Yes," said Henry. "Time to haul bags and boxes into the center."

CHAPTER 6

The Intruder

As the children worked, Mrs. Wickett left the recycling center and went home. Violet noticed that Mrs. Wickett was smiling.

Just as the children finished hauling the last of the boxes into the center and sorting the recycling, they heard a huge boom of thunder.

"Uh-oh," said Jessie. "I don't think we can walk home before the rain comes." Even as Jessie spoke, droplets of rain began to fall from the sky.

Kayla came running up to them. "Better get into my studio," she said. "It's going to pour!"

As the children ran toward the studio with Kayla, they saw Chad running there, too.

Kayla and the Aldens ran into the small shed. Chad ducked into the studio right behind them.

In just that short time, the rain turned from droplets to a heavy downpour.

"It might rain all day," Chad said. "I can give you kids a ride home."

"No, thank you," said Henry. "We'll wait for our Grandfather to get home and pick us up."

"Oh, you shouldn't have to wait all day," said Kayla. "I'll take you home in my van." Kayla handed Jessie her cell phone. "Call your grandfather and tell him that Kayla Korty is giving you a ride home."

Jessie dialed Grandfather, and Grandfather asked to speak to Kayla. Then he asked to speak to Jessie again.

"You can ride with Kayla," said Grandfather. "I know her parents."

Chad turned and walked out into the rain. "If you don't want a ride," he said, "there's no sense in my hanging around. I'll go home, too."

Jessie watched as Kayla used newspaper and cloth to cover up everything on her workbench. Jessie wondered if Kayla was hiding something.

Kayla locked the studio door, and they all ran to her van and piled in. But before Kayla could pull into the street, Chad came running up to them.

"My car won't start," he said. "Can you give me a ride? I don't live far."

"Sure," said Kayla. "Hop in."

By the time Chad squeezed into the van, he was soaked.

"Thanks," he said to Kayla.

"Where to?" she asked him.

"Oh, you can drop the kids off first," he said. "I'm in no hurry."

Jessie thought that Chad had better manners when he needed something, like a ride home.

As Kayla drove the Aldens home, Chad asked them how they became interested in the recycling center. They told him they learned about recycling in school, and that with the help of their grandfather and Mrs. McGregor, they had set up recycling boxes in their garage.

"We used to have to take the newspapers to one town, and the plastics and glass to another," said Henry. "Now we can take everything to one center here in Greenfield."

"You take old newspapers and cans and bottles *to* the center," said Chad, "and you take things home *from* the center."

"Only if we want to," said Jessie.

"We didn't know we could take things home until we saw Mrs. McGregor's big green frog," said Benny.

"Yes," laughed Kayla, "that is one really *big*, really *green* metal frog!" She seemed to think for a while. "I wish I hadn't given that frog away."

"I'm already using the notebooks I took home," said Jessie. She looked down to study

Chad's boots, but the car was so crowded, she couldn't see much.

"What about you, Benny?" Chad asked. "Did you get anything good from the Other Stuff bin?"

"Yes," said Benny. "It's a big red piñata. A bull."

Chad looked out the window. "It's a good thing you rescued it," he said. "The piñata would be ruined if it sat out in the rain. Did you hang the piñata in your bedroom?" he asked.

"No," said Benny. "It's on the sunporch with Mrs. McGregor's frog."

Chad was silent for a while.

"What about you, Chad?" Kayla asked, looking at him through the rearview mirror. "Did you find your pocket watch?"

Chad smiled. "Yes," he said, "I found what I lost."

Soon Kayla pulled into the Aldens' driveway. She drove as close to the house as she could because the rain was still coming down hard.

Henry showed Kayla where to stop. "We'll run in through the sunporch," he said.

The children thanked Kayla for the ride and said good-bye to her and to Chad.

When they got in the house, Mrs. McGregor told the children to change out of their wet shoes and socks. By the time they did that, Grandfather arrived home. Soon it was time for dinner.

At dinner, the children told Grandfather about their day.

"It seems so strange that somebody is breaking into a recycling center," said Grandfather. "They could have anything from it for free."

"We think that two different people have broken in," said Jessie.

"And for two different reasons," said Henry.

* * *

Late that night, when everybody was asleep, Watch began to bark. He barked and barked, louder and louder.

Henry sat up in bed, rubbed his eyes, and listened. He heard the *thump, thump, thump* of Watch's feet.

Benny came running into Henry's room. "Watch is barking," said Benny. "And he is growling."

Henry and Benny ran into the hallway. Jessie and Violet were already there with Grandfather.

They heard more growling from Watch. It was coming from the sunporch.

Grandfather walked into the kitchen and switched on the outdoor lights. The children were behind him.

As soon as the lights went on, they saw somebody running away across their lawn. It looked like a man, but they couldn't be sure.

The children walked into the sunporch with Grandfather. Watch stood at the screen door, barking loudly. The running figure reached the road and disappeared.

Grandfather phoned the police.

"Somebody was trying to get into our house," said Violet.

"But Watch chased the burglar away," said Jessie. She petted Watch. "Good dog," she said. "Good dog."

Henry looked at the screen door, which was still locked on the inside. "Look," he said. "Somebody started to cut a hole in the screen door."

"Watch heard him and chased him away," said Benny. "We are lucky to have Watch."

"We are also lucky to have a strong door between the screen porch and the house," said Grandfather. "I don't think the burglar could have gotten into our house."

Henry grabbed a flashlight from a shelf and opened the screen door.

"What are you doing?" asked Grandfather.

"The ground is wet," said Henry. "I'll bet the intruder left a lot of footprints."

The children and Grandfather and Watch all stepped onto the sidewalk that led up to their screen porch. It didn't take long for

Henry to find a trail of footprints.

One set came toward the screen porch. "That's where he—or she—came up to the house. See how close the footprints are to one another?" asked Henry. "The intruder was walking slowly and quietly."

"Look," said Violet, pointing to a second set of footprints. "Those footprints are going away from the house. They're far apart from one another."

"That means the intruder was running away," said Jessie. "Let me get my notebook."

"Does Jessie want to take notes?" asked Grandfather.

"No," said Henry, "she wants to look at a drawing."

In a minute Jessie was back with one of her new notebooks. She flipped it open, and the children stared at the first footprint drawing she had made.

"No," said Violet. "These footprints are not the same as the first ones we found outside the recycling center."

Jessie flipped the page. "But these footprints are *exactly* the same as the second ones we found outside the recycling center—the ones outside the Other Stuff bin."

Henry, Violet, Benny, and Grandfather all looked at Jessie's second drawing.

"What does it mean?" asked Grandfather.

"I'm not sure, but I have a hunch it means that somebody wants something that was in the Other Stuff recycling bin," said Henry.

CHAPTER 7

One Solution

The next morning, the children had a plan. After breakfast they got on their bikes and pedaled to Tío's Tacos. There they bought six bottles of Doo-Dah Tea: three mint-flavored and three raspberry-flavored.

When they reached the recycling center, they saw Ethan working in the same corner he had worked in before. Once again he was raking up leaves and grass clippings.

When Kayla saw the Aldens, she told them that the recycling center had been broken into again.

"This is so frustrating," Kayla said. "There was no real damage except that the bags of leaves and grass clippings are all broken open. Thank goodness Ethan showed up to volunteer this morning."

The children looked at one another and nodded their heads.

"We know who is breaking into the center and crushing the bags of leaves and grass clippings," Jessie said to Kayla.

"You do?!" Kayla seemed surprised. "Who?"

"We think the person who's doing it wants to tell you himself. And he will, very soon," said Henry.

Kayla looked confused. "Well, okay," she said.

Violet took two bottles of tea out of her bike basket. "Would you like a bottle of tea?" she asked Kayla.

"Oh yes," said Kayla. "Thank you."

And then, to the surprise of the children, Kayla chose a mint-flavored Doo-Dah Tea.

Kayla walked into her studio and the children stood by their bikes for a moment.

"Well," said Jessie at last. "That's a surprise."

"Yes," said Violet. "Yesterday Kayla drank raspberry-flavored tea, but today she chose mint."

"Let's offer Ethan the same choice," said Henry.

The Aldens walked over to where Ethan was raking leaves and grass. They said hello and offered Ethan Doo-Dah Tea.

"No, thanks," said Ethan.

"Kayla is upset," Henry told him. "She's worried about the fact that somebody is getting into the center and opening the bags of leaves and grass."

Ethan shrugged. "She shouldn't be upset, not really. I'm here to clean everything up."

"We would like to show you something," Jessie said to Ethan. "Can you come outside with us for a few minutes?"

Ethan shrugged again, but he put his rake aside. "Sure," he said.

The five of them walked through the gate of the recycling center. Henry led the way. They turned right, then right again.

"Stop," said Henry. They had reached the place just outside the fence from where the bags of leaves and grass were stored.

"The ground is wet," said Jessie. "We're all leaving footprints."

"So?" said Ethan.

Jessie pointed to footprints ahead of them. They were very fresh. The left and right prints were far apart from one another. Both the left and right prints pointed toward the fence.

"Somebody was here before us," she said. "He left footprints, too."

Ethan didn't say anything.

"Look at your footprints," said Henry to Ethan.

Ethan looked down.

"They match those footprints," said Henry, pointing to the prints ahead of them.

Ethan didn't say anything.

"We know what you're doing," Violet said softly.

Ethan shook his head. "Okay," he said. "You're right, those are my footprints. But I'm not really breaking into the recycling center."

"Why are you jumping over the chain-link fence?" Henry asked.

"For fun," said Ethan. "And for training. It's fun and I can keep in shape. I take a running start, jump over the fence, and land on the soft bags of leaves and grass. Nobody knows I can do it except me! And every time I do it, I come in and clean up."

"But when you land on the bags, they break open," said Jessie. "Leaves and grass fall out, and the recycling center looks messy."

"But I come in and clean everything up," Ethan repeated.

"Your kind of fun upsets people," said Violet. "It upsets Kayla because she thinks somebody wants the recycling center to fail."

Ethan looked down at his feet. "Yeah," he said, "I know it's not right. But I was trying to make it right by cleaning up after myself."

The children waited, giving Ethan a chance.

Finally Ethan spoke. "I'll stop doing it," he said. "I guess I have to tell Kayla."

"We'll go with you if you want," said Jessie.

When they walked into Kayla's studio, Henry noticed that she was busy with a soldering torch.

Kayla set the soldering torch aside and removed the magnifying lens she wore on a headband.

"I'm sorry," Ethan said to her. "I won't do it again."

Kayla looked confused. "Huh?" she said.

"I've been jumping over the fence and landing on the bags of leaves and grass clippings," said Ethan. "I'm sorry."

Kayla just stared at him.

"I came in and cleaned up each time I did it," Ethan explained.

"Yes," said Kayla at last. "But all those opened trash bags upset me. I thought somebody didn't like me. I thought they didn't like the recycling center."

"I'm sorry," said Ethan. "I won't do it again."

"But what upsets me even more is that you tipped over the Other Stuff Dumpster," Kayla said. She frowned at Ethan. "You didn't help clean that up."

Ethan looked shocked. "But I didn't do that!" he shouted. "I didn't turn over the Dumpster!"

"Ethan is telling the truth," said Jessie. "He didn't turn over the Dumpster."

Kayla frowned. "You mean to say that two people have been breaking into the recycling center?"

"Yes," said Henry. "And the break-ins aren't the only crime to solve."

"They aren't?" asked Kayla. "What else is there?"

Jessie spoke. "Somebody robbed Jonah's Jewelry Store three weeks ago. They stole a bag of diamonds."

"Diamonds?" Kayla seemed nervous. "I don't know anything about diamonds."

Jessie thought Kayla's comment was strange. *Nobody is accusing her of taking the diamonds,* thought Jessie. *Why does she act guilty?*

"We think that the diamond theft and the second break-in here might be connected," Jessie explained.

"No," said Kayla, standing up. "That's ridiculous. There's no connection between the robbery and the recycling center."

The Aldens and Ethan watched as Kayla shoved all her pieces of metal and sparkling glass into a drawer. Then she shut the drawer and locked it.

"You kids might be able to figure out who turned over the Other Stuff Dumpster," she said. "I hope you do. But you won't be able to solve who stole the diamonds."

"We will solve it," said Henry.

"No," said Kayla. "If the police haven't solved it, you won't, either."

The children turned to leave, but Kayla stopped them. "Wait," she said. "This morning I found something in the Other Stuff bin: something just for Violet."

Kayla rummaged around under one of her benches, then pulled out something wrapped in plastic. Kayla removed the plastic and the children saw a large piece of beautiful purple cloth.

Kayla handed the cloth to Violet. "Somebody left this brand new cloth in the Other Stuff bin."

Violet held the cloth, which shimmered with flecks of gold. She saw that there were thin gold-colored threads woven through the cloth. "It's so pretty," said Violet. The cloth felt very soft and smooth in her hands.

Violet smiled. "Thank you," she said. "I don't see how anybody could give away something purple."

CHAPTER 8

The Bottom of the Boots

The children stood just outside the gate to the recycling center. Ethan had gone back to work on the bags, and Kayla was in her studio.

"We know that Ethan didn't climb the fence and tip over the Other Stuff Dumpster," said Violet.

"Because his footprints don't match the smaller set of footprints," said Jessie.

"And because Ethan could *jump* over the fence," said Benny. "But the person who tipped the Dumpster had to *climb* over."

"We need to find out whose footprints match the second set," said Henry. "Then we need to find out why that person tipped over the Dumpster."

The children stood there and thought.

"We need to see the tread marks on Mrs. Wickett's shoes, on Chad's shoes, and even on Kayla's shoes," said Jessie at last.

Her brothers and sister agreed.

"Look!" said Benny, pointing across the street. "I just saw something bright red. I think it's Mrs. Wickett's boots!"

The Aldens crossed the street and walked into Mrs. Wickett's yard. They walked around the back, where Benny had seen something red. There was Mrs. Wickett, kneeling in her garden. She wore an old jacket and pants and her bright red boots.

"Oh, hello," she said when she saw them. "What a nice surprise."

The children said hello.

Benny noticed that the bottom of Mrs. Wickett's boots were facing out, so he bent down to look at them.

As soon as she saw what Benny was doing, Mrs. Wickett scooted around so that Benny couldn't see her boots. Then she stood up.

"Why don't we all go and sit on my front porch?" she said. "I'm done gardening for the day."

Once everybody was settled on the front porch, Mrs. Wickett offered them lemonade. All four children accepted.

"This is delicious," said Violet as she sipped her glass of lemonade.

Mrs. Wickett smiled. "Thank you," she said. "I made it myself."

Then Mrs. Wickett sat in a wicker chair. "Well," she said, "what has Kayla decided to do about all the recycling that people leave alongside the sidewalk?"

"We don't know," said Jessie. "She hasn't said."

"We think Kayla should leave the center open until midnight," said Henry. "But she won't. She says she's worried about people breaking into her studio."

"Kayla makes lovely jewelry out of junk,"

said Mrs. Wickett, sipping her lemonade. "She brought some of it to Jonah's Jewelry Store and asked Mr. Jonah if he would sell it."

"Kayla told us about that," said Violet. "But Mr. Jonah said no."

"That's right," Mrs. Wicket said. "Mr. Jonah doesn't like jewelry made out of recycled metals and glass. I'm afraid he said some very insulting things to Kayla."

"When was this?" asked Henry.

"Oh, a few weeks ago. A day or two before the robbery," Mrs. Wickett answered.

The children looked at one another.

"Mrs. Wickett," said Jessie, "do you want the recycling center to fail?"

Instead of answering, Mrs. Wickett sipped her lemonade and stared across the street at the recycling center. Finally she spoke. "Recycling is a good thing," she said. "But bags of recycling outside the recycling center are not a good thing. I just don't know."

"Somebody climbed over the fence and tipped over the Other Stuff Dumpster," said

Henry. "Did you do that?"

"My word!" exclaimed Mrs. Wickett. "You children do ask direct questions, don't you?"

Henry waited for an answer.

"No, I did not," Mrs. Wickett replied.

"We found footprints outside the fence, where somebody climbed over," said Jessie. She took out her notebook. "I made a drawing of the footprints."

Mrs. Wickett didn't say anything.

"May we see the bottom of your red boots?" Henry asked.

Mrs. Wickett stood up. "No, you may not!" she said.

"Why won't you let us see them?" asked Benny.

"I am innocent!" Mrs. Wickett shouted. "I don't have to prove I'm innocent—you have to prove I'm guilty!" She marched into her house and slammed the door.

* * *

Once again, the children returned to the front gate of the recycling center.

"We are down to two suspects for the second break-in," said Violet. "The break-in where somebody tipped over the Other Stuff Dumpster. It was either Chad or Mrs. Wickett."

"But we have three suspects for the diamond robbery," said Jessie. "It's either Chad, Mrs. Wickett, or Kayla."

"We might have two separate crimes to solve," said Henry. "Or the two crimes might be connected."

"I think the crimes are connected," said Violet.

Everybody else agreed with Violet.

"That means the diamonds are hidden somewhere in the recycling center," said Henry. "Or they *were* hidden there, and now they're somewhere else."

Benny had been thinking hard, and now he spoke up. "I think the diamonds were hidden in the Other Stuff bin," he said.

Henry smiled at his younger brother. "Not

in the bin itself," said Henry, "but *inside* something that was in the bin."

"Not inside of Mrs. McGregor's green frog," said Violet. "That's made of metal and has no place to hide anything."

"Not inside my notebooks," said Jessie.

"*Ohhhhhh,*" said Benny as he figured it out. "The diamonds are hidden inside my piñata!" Benny thought about this for a moment. "But how did they get there?" he asked.

"I think that whoever robbed Jonah's Jewelry Store went to Tío's Tacos late at night," said Henry. "And when there weren't any other customers, the thief put the diamonds into the piñata."

"But why?" asked Jessie. "Why didn't the thief just take the jewels home?"

"I've been thinking about that," said Henry. "Whoever stole the diamonds must have been afraid of being searched. Or of having their house searched."

This made sense to Jessie. Tío's piñatas were all hanging from the ceiling. Nobody ever touched them. "Tío's piñatas are a pretty safe place to store diamonds," she said. "They just hang from the ceiling and get old and dusty."

"The thief didn't know that Tío was going to replace the old piñatas with new ones," said Henry.

The children decided it was time to go home and make a plan. They rode their bikes home, put them away, and sat in the sunporch.

"Let's open the piñata and take out the diamonds," said Benny.

"Not yet," said Henry. "We can look inside the piñata later. Let's think first."

Everybody looked at Henry.

"Maybe we can leave the piñata where it is and use it to trap the thief," Henry said.

"How?" asked Jessie.

"I don't know," said Henry.

Benny looked at his red piñata, which was still hanging from the ceiling of the sunporch. "My bull piñata looks lonesome," he said.

Violet sat right up. "Benny!" she said. "That's it! What a brilliant idea!"

"Huh?" said Benny. "What idea?"

"Your piñata is lonesome, so we'll have a *party* for it!" said Violet. She reached up and took the piñata down from the ceiling.

Henry liked the way Violet was thinking.

"We'll invite Kayla and Mrs. Wickett and Chad," he said. "One of them will really, *really* want the piñata."

"Let's invite Ethan, too," said Jessie, "even though we know he didn't steal the diamonds."

"And let's invite Tío," said Violet. "That way, we can make sure that Benny's piñata really is from Tío's Tacos."

The children went to talk to Mrs. McGregor and Grandfather, both of whom agreed a party was a good idea.

"Let's have it tomorrow afternoon," said Henry.

"I'll set up the badminton," said Jessie.

Benny liked to push croquet wickets into the ground, so he volunteered to set up the croquet game. And Violet loved putting out paper plates, cups, and napkins. *And I have a perfect use for all that purple cloth*, she thought.

After the children planned everything with Mrs. McGregor and Grandfather, they called Kayla to invite her to the party. Then they called Mrs. Wickett and invited her. They asked her if she would invite Chad, and she said Chad was visiting with her, so she would ask him. Finally, they called Ethan and Tío and invited them, too.

"Everything is set," said Jessie, "Now it's notebook time."

CHAPTER 9

Notebook Time

That evening, the children were in Jessie's bedroom for notebook time. Notebook time was when they talked about their clues. Jessie, who loved making lists, wrote everything into her notebook. Talking things out always helped the children think more clearly. Benny lay on the bed. Henry and Violet sat on the floor. Jessie sat at her desk.

"I'll use one of my brand-new notebooks to list what we know," said Jessie. "Using a notebook we rescued from the trash pile seems right, doesn't it?"

Everybody agreed.

Jessie began her list. "Let's start with Chad," she said.

"He worked at Jonah's Jewelry Store," said Violet. "So he knew where the diamonds were."

"Yes," said Henry. "And he quit working at Jonah's Jewelry Store the day after the robbery. I wonder why?"

Benny's eyes had started to close, but suddenly he was wide awake. "Chad might eat at Tío's Tacos," he said. "If he does, he would know there are piñatas there!"

"And Chad was looking for something in the recycling center," said Violet. "He said he was looking for a pocket watch. But I didn't believe him."

Benny started to fall asleep again.

"I think Mrs. Wickett didn't believe him, either," said Henry. "She said she had never seen him with a pocket watch. Maybe he was looking for the piñata."

"What about footprints?" Jessie asked.

"Hmmm," said Henry. "We never had a chance to check the bottom of Chad's boots to see if he's the person who broke into the recycling center."

Once again Benny woke up. "Chad drinks mint-flavored tea," he mumbled.

"Is that suspicious?" asked Henry.

Jessie smiled because she knew what Benny meant. When she and Benny were putting things into the correct bins the first day, Benny found a mint Doo-Dah Tea bottle inside the glass recycling bin. Jessie explained this to Henry and Violet, who had been working near the gate at the time.

"So," asked Henry, "you're thinking that Chad climbed the fence and drank some tea and then just tossed the bottle in the closest bin?"

Benny didn't answer because this time, Benny was sound asleep.

"I'm not sure somebody would keep a bottle of tea in his pocket while he climbed a fence," said Violet.

Henry agreed that this was not likely. "But *not likely* doesn't mean impossible," he reminded his sisters.

"There's one other thing about Chad," said Jessie. "He was in the car when Kayla dropped us off on the day it rained. So he knows where we live. And that night, somebody tried to break into the sunporch."

After they finished discussing Chad, Jessie wrote on one of the pages of her new notebook:

Chad:
—worked at Jonah's Jewelry
—might eat at Tío's Tacos
—was looking for something in the recycling center
—knew that the piñata was in the sunporch

"There's somebody else who knows that the piñata is in our sunporch," said Henry.

"Yes," said Jessie. "Kayla knows because she drove us home."

"According to Mrs. Wickett, Kayla was angry with Mr. Jonah because he wouldn't carry her jewelry," said Henry. "Maybe she stole his diamonds because she was angry."

Jessie tapped her pencil against her notebook. "We saw Kayla reading the newspaper article about the diamond theft," she said. "And then she turned the newspaper over."

"Not only that," said Henry, "but Kayla locks all her glass stones in a drawer each night. Why would you lock up glass stones?"

Jessie was thinking the same thing. "Do we know for sure that they're glass, not diamonds?" she asked.

"Chad said the stone in my key ring is glass," said Henry. "He worked in a jewelry store, so he should know."

Violet spoke up. "Mrs. Wickett works in a jewelry store, too. She looked at the stone in your key ring, but she never said it was glass. She never said it was a diamond, either."

"That's right," said Henry. He looked at his key ring. "If this is a real diamond, then I got a real bargain."

Henry, Jessie, and Violet laughed.

That woke Benny up. "Who are we making a list about?" he asked.

"Kayla," said Jessie.

Benny sat up and rubbed his eyes. "But Kayla wouldn't climb the fence and tip over her own Dumpster. She has a key!"

"That's true," said Henry, "but maybe Kayla wants it to look like somebody is breaking in."

"Why would she do that?" Violet asked.

Henry didn't know, so he just shrugged.

"Does Kayla eat at Tío's?" Benny asked.

Nobody knew the answer to that question. Jessie wrote:

> **Kayla:**
> —is angry at Jonah's Jewelry
> —hides her recycled jewelry and sparkling stones
> —knows that the piñata is in the sunporch
> —might eat at Tío's Tacos, but we don't know

"That leaves Mrs. Wickett," said Benny. "I like her red boots. They're as red as my bull piñata. But," he added, "she wouldn't let us see the bottoms."

"Mrs. Wickett works at Jonah's Jewelry Store, and she works there at night," said Jessie.

"Yes," said Violet. "The robbery took place at night, around midnight. Mrs. Wickett could have taken the jewels straight to Tío's Tacos."

"We know she eats at Tío's Tacos," said Jessie.

Henry was still looking at the stone in his key ring. Finally he put it away. "It seems like Mrs. Wickett wants the recycling center to fail," he said. "Could she have stolen the diamonds and planted them in the center to blame Kayla?"

Jessie tapped her pencil. "Maybe," she said. "But that's not likely."

Henry agreed that it wasn't likely. "She's friends with Chad," he said. "Maybe the two of them worked together to steal the diamonds. And," he added, "Chad was visiting her when we called to invite her to the party."

Jessie wrote in her new notebook:

Mrs. Wickett:

—works at Jonah's Jewelry Store

—works at night, when the jewels were stolen

—eats at Tío's Tacos

—is friends with Chad, who also worked at Jonah's Jewelry Store

After Jessie read the list, Benny added something. "Mrs. Wickett didn't know where we live," he said.

"Maybe Chad told her where we live," said Jessie.

CHAPTER 10

The Diamond Thief

The next afternoon was bright and sunny as the children welcomed people to their party. Grandfather was there, of course, and so was Mrs. McGregor. Tío brought some delicious food along with him. Chad arrived with Mrs. Wickett. Watch growled at both of them. Kayla came with Ethan. She kept staring at the green metal frog.

Everybody helped themselves to lemonade or iced tea, then they all played games. Ethan and Jessie paired up to play badminton. So did Henry and Chad. Benny watched to call the birdie fair or foul.

It looked as if Kayla was going to win at croquet, but Mrs. Wickett wound up winning.

After games, the children and their guests gathered around to talk. Henry, Benny, and Chad stood around the grill where Tío helping Mrs. McGregor prepare more food.

"Did you see Kayla looking at that green frog?" Chad asked. "I think she wants it back."

"No," said Henry, "I think she's just happy the frog has a home."

Chad looked at the bull piñata that was still hanging in the sunporch. "I wanted that piñata," he told Benny. "But you got to it first."

"*Sí,*" said Tío as he cooked. "That is one of my old piñatas. Chad came in one morning and was very upset when the old piñatas were gone. I told him I took them to the recycling center."

"That piñata would look great in my den," Chad said to Benny. "I'd like to buy it from you." Chad pulled out his wallet. "How much do you want?" he asked.

Benny shook his head. "I don't want to sell my piñata. I want to break it open."

Tío laughed. "Benny is right," he said. "This is a party. It is a good time to break open a piñata! I hope somebody stuffed the piñata with good things. You must always put good things into a piñata—shiny half-dollars, wrapped cookies, things like that."

Chad frowned. "If you break it open, you ruin the piñata."

"Then I'll get another one," said Benny, "and we'll have another party!"

Jessie and Violet stayed with Kayla, Ethan, and Mrs. Wickett. Violet noticed that both Kayla and Mrs. Wickett were wearing sparkling stones.

"I have a great idea," Kayla told Mrs. Wickett.

"What's that?" asked Mrs. Wickett.

"I know how we can solve the problem of the recycling bags and boxes that people leave outside the gate every night," said Kayla.

Jessie and Violet were very glad to hear that Kayla wanted to solve this problem.

"I want to hire you," Kayla said to Mrs. Wickett. "I want to hire you to keep the center open from five o'clock in the afternoon until midnight. That way, people can drive into the center and sort all of their recycling or drop it off alongside one of the Dumpsters."

Mrs. Wickett thought about this. "That way, there won't be any trash outside the recycling center. I won't have to look at it all the time." She frowned. "But I already have a job. I work at Jonah's Jewelry Store in the evenings."

"Oh," said Kayla. She seemed disappointed. "I was really hoping you would say yes."

"Hmmm," said Mrs. Wickett as she sipped iced tea. "I like your idea. I think recycling is important. But Mr. Jonah gives me a big discount on jewelry," she said. "If he didn't, I couldn't afford to wear these diamonds."

Kayla looked at the rings. "If you worked at the recycling center, you could make your own rings. I try to keep my designs secret until I'm ready to sell them," said Kayla, "but I can show them to you."

"Is that why you cover up your jewelry when people walk into your studio?" asked Violet.

"Yes," said Kayla. "I don't like people to see my art until it's finished."

Suddenly Mrs. Wickett smiled. "Yes!" she told Kayla. "I'll take the job. I'll keep the recycling center open until midnight. And I'll learn how to recycle junk into jewelry!"

Kayla smiled as she and Mrs. Wickett shook hands.

Jessie and Violet smiled, too.

Then everybody helped themselves to the wonderful food that Tío and Mrs. McGregor had prepared. All the food was laid out in bright dishes on the new purple tablecloth that Violet had made from the cloth Kayla had found in the Other Stuff bin.

Each person found a lawn chair or blanket to sit on while eating.

After everybody finished, Henry stood up and announced that it was time to swing at the piñata and see what kind of prizes fell out.

The guests followed Henry into the sunporch. Violet gave each guest a purple blindfold. She had also made these from the cloth Kayla had given her.

"Benny will go first," said Tío as he tied the blindfold around Benny. "Here is the stick," he said, putting a sturdy stick in Benny's hand.

But before Benny could swing at the piñata, Chad pushed him away, pulled the piñata off the ceiling, and ran out the door.

"Hey!" shouted Ethan. "You pushed Benny!"

Ethan and Henry both ran after Chad, but Ethan was faster.

Ethan tackled Chad. The piñata flew out of Chad's hands and onto the lawn.

Everybody rushed out and surrounded Chad and Ethan.

"That was a terrible thing to do," Mrs. Wickett said to Chad. "What is wrong with you?"

Henry picked up the piñata. "I think Chad

wants something that's inside this piñata," he said. "But it's not in there anymore. We took it out before we could swing at the piñata." Henry reached into his pocket. He pulled out a small brown cloth bag. "Are you looking for this?" he asked Chad.

Mrs. Wickett gasped. "That's a Jonah's Jewelry Store bag! Those are the stolen diamonds!"

"Let me up," said Chad. "I can explain."

Ethan let Chad stand up—but as soon as Chad stood, he raced away toward the street.

"Let him go," Henry told Ethan.

All the guests watched as two men stepped out of a car that had been parked alongside the street. They grabbed Chad and hand-cuffed him.

"Oh," said Mrs. Wickett to Grandfather. "Do you always have unmarked police cars parked on your street?"

Grandfather chuckled. "No," he admitted, "but I called them before the party to let them know that the diamond thief would be at the party."

Mrs. Wickett looked at Henry, Jessie, Violet, and Benny. "You must have great confidence in your grandchildren," she said.

"Yes," said Grandfather proudly. "They know right from wrong."

Mrs. Wickett looked at the children again. "I'm sorry that I wouldn't let you see the bottom of my boots," she said. "They are very old and shabby. I didn't want you to see that there are holes in the bottom."

"Oh, Mrs. Wickett," said Kayla. "Old and shabby can be very good."

Mrs. Wickett smiled. "Yes," she said, "I suppose I could give you the boots and you would find a use for them."

Kayla smiled and nodded.

Tío spoke up. "So tell me, how did the diamonds get into my piñata, which is now Benny's piñata?"

"Well," said Jessie, "we figure that the night Chad stole the diamonds, he went across the street to your restaurant. Then, when you were back in the kitchen and there was nobody around, he put the bag of diamonds into the piñata."

Tío rubbed his chin. "Chad was a customer that night," he said. "And there was nobody else there. And I *did* go into the kitchen."

Tío thought some more. "That explains why when Chad came in again last week, he was very upset that the piñatas were gone."

One of the police officers pushed Chad into the car. The other officer came up to the guests.

"Here are the diamonds," said Henry, handing the bag to the officer.

The police officer looked inside the bag. Everybody could see the sparkling stones. He closed the bag, nodded to everybody, and walked back to his car.

"Wow!" said Kayla. "I guess what I'm always saying is true—there are treasures in recycling!"

"Yes," said Benny, picking up his piñata. "But you can't eat diamonds. Piñatas should be stuffed with things you can eat!"